# LIFE OF A
# BIKER CHICK
## GOOD GIRL/BAD GURL II

by

# SUNRIZE JACKSON

**Life of a Biker Chick**
**Good Girl/Bad Gurl II**
*by*
**Sunrize Jackson**

Contact the author at:

Email:     sunrizeflavor@gmail.com
Website:   www.goodgirlbadgurl.com
Facebook:  Author Sunrize Jackson

Cover Design: JL Promotions

Editing:   Gloria Palmer (movinonup57@yahoo.com)

ISBN-13:   978-1-5136-5029-6

This book is printed on acid-free paper.

## Acknowledgements

To my three girls—Erica, Aaliyah, and Paress—I am hoping you share and take heed of the mistakes I made and do better . . .

## Dedications

Thanking every one of you who supported me and stood by me when no one else would: Marland, Tewana, Carla, Danielle, Shawnie, Joyce, Tiffany, Dathan, all my roadies!!

To my biker family: I love each and every one of you!!

To my sister Hollywood, who inspired me to write this book.

Syncere, thank you for dealing with me all year. Your faith and belief helped me with my spiritual growth.

# LIFE OF A
# BIKER CHICK
## GOOD GIRL/BAD GURL II

# CHAPTER 1

It took Mya eight years to relocate from Milwaukee to Belleview to Memphis—where she met Fred, her second husband—before she came back to Milwaukee, separating herself from a marriage she'd lost her identity in and become a miserable wife who had been cheated on and emotionally tortured.

After she lost Kyle, her brother, to police violence, her old buddy Candy, who she called sister, had reached out and given her a job working under her in the corporate world. Candy had climbed her way to the top and Mya was happy for her. They were old friends from back when Mya had first come to Milwaukee. Unfortunately, Mya had left and moved back to the south. Candy had always been labeled as Mya's ride-or-die chick.

Candy was a party girl and loved to club and bar hop, which was the best way to get some of her time because she was always busy. Mya knew she had some country ways, but she was so appreciative of Candy helping and giving her an opportunity to get out of a situation that she rose to every occasion to be there whenever Candy needed her. However, she was extremely bored with the whole 'sit around the bar scene' with people who often did not talk to her that she craved to do something different.

At this time in her life, Mya didn't have a specific set of friends. Usually, she'd meet people all the time, but somehow it seemed now that she was always hanging with a friend who always brought other friends who Mya really didn't know well. So, she started meeting up with her old friend from her hometown, Nette, who always seemed to be doing something interesting.

She was also dealing with the fact that Mr. Brown, her dad, was dying of heart failure and cancer. Mya really needed to find an outlet to deal with the pain. She was the only girl, and the youngest, with three brothers. Mr. Brown and Mya's brothers had taught her to be tough and how to ride mini-bikes, go-carts, and to drive Mr. Brown's old trucks and vans. Mya was a tomboy in her own way right from the start. Mr. Brown and Mya were so close, and she dreaded all the pain he felt as each day went by and she had to talk to Mrs. Brown about his condition. Mya's heart was collapsing. She felt she really had no one to talk with or maybe no one who would be sensitive enough to listen.

On the first day with Nette, she and her friends took Mya to a bar where bikers hung out. That was her very first encounter at a biker set. Mya's eyes were big and bright as she watched the bikers pass by or she watched them looking at her. She watched in amazement how they pulled up on their motorcycles and parked. Some of them had some beautiful bikes, and some of them were so different that a person would have to see them for themselves to appreciate them. She pictured herself riding right then and there.

Some of the vested bikers were friendly, some were not; some had long beards, long trench coats; and some were dripped down in biker gear from head to toe. The most important thing they wanted to know was, "Who did Mya come here with?" See, a person not flying colors just couldn't appear at these settings unless they knew you or you had come with someone they knew. So, after a few times going to biker sets, she began to meet a few people and a some were getting comfortable with her coming around.

The first two men she met were P-Town and Racer. P-Town was a flashy, preppy-looking dude who smiled about anything. Racer was the total opposite. He looked like a biker and wore his biker T-shirts and denims, and was grouchy for the most part, unless he was laughing at some of the humorous insults he gave to just about anyone who approached him. P-Town always greeted Mya when he saw her, which made her feel accepted on the bike scene. Racer was quiet most times with her but decided one day to ask her to ride on the back of his bike.

"Hey lady, we're goin' over to Blues. You wanna ride with me?" he asked.

"Yeeesss, I sure would! How do I get on?" she asked.

"Put your feet on the pegs and hold on; that's about it."

He laughed, put his cigar out, and began to start the bike. Mya got on happily with a big grin on her face. As Nette and her friends yelled at him, "YOU'D BE CAREFUL WITH HER!," they headed off. The ride was so smooth that all she could do was relax her mind and think about Mr. Brown, but the ride caused her be at peace instead of feeling like crying or yelling. Then they pulled into the bar called Blues.

"How d'you like it?" Racer asked.

Mya nodded. Racer had a sport bike and was known to ride it pretty fast, but since he had a newbie on his bike, he gave Mya a nice, smooth ride. After that, she would catch a ride with him if he was headed to the same places as Nette and her friends. During some of those rides, she shared with him about Mr. Brown's condition. Racer told her to keep herself entertained at this time. He knew it was critical for Mya to stay around friends and people who cared. He told her to embrace the biker scene and the pain she was dealing with would be soothed much easier.

Although Mya didn't know Racer that well, she accepted the advice and came around even more. Just about three nights out the week, they visited biker sets which made the pain Mya was feeling from dealing with the fact that Mr. Brown was going to eventually leave her a little more bearable.

Mya spent a lot of time going back and forth to Belleview to check on her dad's condition. Each and every time he would say something that would affect her internally. Mr. Brown had told Mya stories of the animals and how to watch them in nature, how obedient they were to God. He told Mya she was an eagle.

"Stay up," he said. "Don't come down with the sparrows," he finished.

He even told Mya he couldn't live surrounded with four walls, not being able to go anywhere. "I want you to be strong, Mya, and don't come back here."

Mya was so distraught. She knew she wouldn't have her number-one man in her life much longer. A couple of months later, she lost Mr. Brown. He was gone and she was torn apart. She felt like she had no one. Mr. Brown was the only man she'd respected. He was truly the only man that she knew cared for and loved her, the only man she knew who'd never abused her in any way. The only man who'd taught her to stand up for anything she felt she should. She was his baby girl.

Racer checked up on her while she was down south burying Mr. Brown and made sure she knew someone cared. Nette was there with her and attended Mr. Brown's funeral, while her friends called and told her how much they knew she was hurting. Nette kept bringing up the question of if she was interested in joining a social club. Now, if you don't know what a social club is, it's a group or club of ladies or men, or it's coed, who don't ride motorcycles but they support the motorcycle riders, do charities, and learn to come together like a family. She told Mya she would find a better day to discuss this with her. Too late; she had her attention now.

She felt a little bit unsure about joining because it was something she had never done. She was worried about how her other friends and family were going to react. Mya mostly wondered how Mrs. Brown, her mother, would feel about her joining. By this time, Mrs. Brown was a retired judge and a deacon's wife who sat on the mother board and belonged to a few organizations in the small town Mya had come from. Here she was about to embark on something most people might not ever understand, so she had a talk with her mother who told her she was glad she'd found something to keep her active and at least they were having organized fun. She could remember when Mya was heavy in the nightclubs and some of the encounters she'd experienced.

After Mya came back from burying her dad, she began to pick up the pieces of her life and tried to stay motivated. She met with Nette and a group of women who all were part of the social club she wanted to join. There were about nine or ten career-minded women in the room with smiles on their faces as she entered. They came up with a club name of Choir Angels. Bambi, a big, stout, strong-looking woman, and a friend of Nette's, was the president, and they asked Nette to become their new vice president. She had not seen any of these women on the motorcycle scene when she was hanging out with Nette or Bambi. They gave Mya the biker name of Lady M. The other members were Hollywood, Laffy, Butta, Rat Girl, Buffy, Dynamite, and Lil Secret.

Mya had not run this by her friend Racer, who she knew would be mad because he liked to enlighten her on things when it came to the bike scene. Nette told Mya to keep it a secret until they officially came out with their colors on. Colors were the centerpiece on a patch which were a symbol of who they were or what their club was.

Luckily, she convinced Candy and her sister—who they called Sister—to join, and they gave her a biker name of Nanny, while Candy used Carmel. She also had a co-worker who came in and named herself Foxy Loxy, who Mya insisted be the treasurer. She really didn't know what to expect, how a meeting like this worked, or anything about a social club. Reality was she had stumbled upon something new, and so far, she was ready to see what lay ahead.

# CHAPTER 2

Their first night out as members was crazy. They went to an annual dance at a biker club in the city. They all showed up and walked in together. Bambi, their president, had explained to them how important it was for them to do this and the fact that she would fine them if they weren't on time. As they walked in together, their exterior came across their faces as they knew this would be a shock to almost everyone. Some got into beast mode and some got in diva mode as they entered.

The truth was out, and Racer, P-Town, and everyone else who knew them realized at that moment they had formed a club and become part of the motorcycle scene. A lot of the men welcomed them and a lot of the women did not. It always took a while for the women to warm up to anything, especially new women. This was not a great feeling, but like Bambi had told them, you will be tested on your loyalty and strength. This is not for everyone or every female.

Bambi had also preached how important it was to form a sisterhood between them. She was hard on them and made sure they understood that sometimes people on the motorcycle scene would try to work them against one another. Like a mother, she wanted them to bond like sisters. For example, one day they all would be out, having a great time together, and one biker would be asking one of the girls in the club out, totally seeming he was really into her. The next night, he would be after the next one in the same club. Only a few of them weren't bending like that. It was really dependent on the type of women you had in the club because some women were so happy that a man was adoring them and making them feel pretty or special that she would forget all about her sisters in the club in the blink of an eye. Some women came for respect, some didn't; some never came to learn anything, but most were there for the attention. All of them had an agenda. Women come from all different types of lifestyles and places, and it is sometimes hard to line them all up on the same page.

Bambi was sometimes hard to deal with, and she definitely had to babysit half the women on a daily. Dealing with Bambi's loud mouth and cursing reminded Mya of her mother and she felt right at home. Mya's mother never tolerated disobedient children, everyone knew she meant business, so Bambi to Mya was like a walk in the park compared to Mrs. Brown.

Eventually, Mya took on the role of secretary and grew stronger along with Bambi. She watched and listened to a lot of her arguments and issues on the motorcycle scene. Bambi did not allow anyone to disrespect her, her man, or her members. Bambi was quick with her tongue lashing and didn't mind backing up every bit of what she said. She would even beat a man if he let her get close enough. Mya began to understand why she had to be this way.

Mya had come from domestic violence issues, with men being disrespectful, so seeing Bambi handling men that way made Mya step it up. It was important for Bambi to relay to the biker world that they were a club, starting from the top, and they wanted to be recognized as ladies, not just a bunch of "floozies or groupies". She took that stand and made it very clear, but some of the fellow members didn't like it so well. They complained a lot and would really look pitiful if they couldn't get loose.

Taking the role of secretary, she helped form and change their by-laws and their rules to fit the unnecessary drama women brought to the club, such as: screwing the same men, fighting over attention, fighting over disrespect issues, and shameful drunkenness. Mya grew more into her role of secretary and followed her president as directed when needed.

The Choir Angels found a bar to hold their own set, and every week on that night, a lot of bikers supported them as they (Nette and Bambi) had done for other clubs on their nights. They fed their fellow brothers and sisters on that night and had a lot of fun. It was always exciting when they could all party together and dance the night away, forgetting about the fact that most of the women had children at home to attend to and they had to get them up for school the next morning.

Mya had two girls, Desiree, who'd come from her marriage to Michael, and Katy, who'd come from her marriage to Fred. Desiree had turned fourteen and Katy was three, but somehow, she managed to make it work. It took members to participate to make it work; that much Mya understood.

For the first couple of months, there wasn't any drama on their set night, but within their club, there were problems with participation. Women couldn't make it due to babysitting or boyfriend problems. There also were problems with members being late and attitudes, and negativity began to surface.

"To be part of this world, there are sacrifices to be made if you plan on participating," Bambi often stated.

Mya had begun to drink a lot more, keeping a bottle in her vest when she attended most of the set nights, or she made sure she stopped at the bar counter first after she greeted her fellow biker family. She was always ready to argue with just about anybody and stayed ready for unnecessary issues, especially when the members needed her.

The craziest part was that some of her own members were the ones who began to talk about her and whisper behind her back. There was even an altercation where a member asked Mya to buy her a drink. When Mya told her she wasn't buying drinks, that was why she'd brought hers with her, she got so mad that she told Mya, "That's why you need to watch your back." Shocked this had come out her mouth, Mya felt maybe she should just take her out now! She grabbed her by the neck and tried to choke her to death.

Mya told her, "I got you! I don't need anyone else."

As she choked the member, Nanny, Candy's older sister who also was in the club, put her hand on Mya's shoulder and asked her to release her.

"That's enough," she said as she patted Mya's shoulder. "That's enough."

Mya admitted then that women change when they were around a group of men. These women in the club had gotten crazy. Mya thought they were supposed to be at least respectful to one another, but since she didn't buy her a drink, somehow she was the one who was in the wrong. Mya left out the door quickly after that and planted herself in the car in disbelief of how wrong that situation had gone.

"Maybe this isn't for me," she wondered to herself.

# CHAPTER 3

Mya prided herself in never being a quitter and she really wanted to see this thing through, so she swallowed how she really felt and waited a few days before she came back around her club sisters again. The next set night she decided to show up, Mya came with Candy and they stayed off to themselves. Candy asked whether they should call it quits. Mya shook her head no.

"The next one's just gon catch it, that's all," she replied.

The club went a whole two weeks without any problems, until a member Mya had referred named Starlight was upset with the president and VP. This member took it to a whole other level by bringing in some of her family members and demanding a refund of her membership dues. The club members stood up to watch them march to the back where their president and VP stood and to see what was going on.

"We'd better check to make sure your girl Nette isn't in any trouble," Candy said.

They began to position themselves, walking toward the back. They noticed a few of the women who'd come had bats, pipes, and brass knuckles, so they stood behind them. This situation did not look too pretty. Starlight (the member who was demanding a refund) began snapping off to Bambi and Nette. This was a big deal on the bike scene because no one should ever be able to approach your leaders like that. They began to get closer and push back the unwelcomed women. Suddenly, Mya heard her name.

"MYA!"

It was Bambi.

'Now why would she call me by my government?' she thought.

"We have a problem. You're the one who referred Starlight!" said Bambi.

Mya couldn't believe she'd just yelled out her government name or the fact she'd yelled it out in the clubhouse around so many other bikers. Mya was angry and they began to step to each other. Bambi rolled her neck and kept snapping repeatedly, "We're gon take this up in the meeting!"

Mya began to snap back, when Candy grabbed her. "Let's go! We don't have time for this!" she said, pointing toward the door. As they began to walk out, Mya knew she was done with the Choir Angels.

Immediately, she began to separate herself from the club after the situation with Starlight. She went to the functions with no happiness; she had no enthusiasm and didn't entertain anything from her co-members. She believed, after that situation, that many people came to their set nights just to see who would act up or who was going to get into it with whom. It was funny like that.

One club of all men hung around them more than the rest; they called themselves Dangerous Wind. They made sure they supported them so hard that they moved when the Choir Angels moved and the Choir Angels moved when they moved, supporting them just the same. Every one of these men liked someone in the club, whether they said it or they just smiled so hard that you saw the attraction in their smile.

One member named Rooster had his eye on Mya. He was tall and slim with a nice Charlie Brown haircut. Rooster had the prettiest eyes and he knew it the way he used them to stare at Mya. He had begun to sit down by her every time they came around one another to hold a conversation. Their conversations grew stronger each time and began to get a little deeper. They talked a lot about their kids and life outside the motorcycle scene, until finally they decided to go on a date.

When news got back to Racer, he wasn't happy. "Does this dude have a bike, sis?"

She put her head down and answered, "No."

"Then, heck no! That's gonna make you look bad!" he snapped.

Mya couldn't believe what Racer had said. What was she gonna do? She had already started to like Rooster.

# CHAPTER 4

One day, the treasurer, Foxy Loxy, decided to enlighten the club on how the president and vice president had been forcing her to give them the club's money. One minute, the club had money; the next minute, it all was gone—each of them blaming the other. There was so much going on at one time that Mya couldn't think straight. It was beginning to be too much for her to take in, so she decided to take a short vacation home to visit her mom. She had a plan that, once she returned, she would know what she wanted to do concerning the club—whether she wanted to go or stay.

### At Momma's House ~

"I tell you, baby, even in church, we have rules of organization, and that money business has a big sign on it saying, 'Goodbye!'" said Mrs. Brown as she puffed on her cigarette.

Mya nodded her head to agree. "I know, Momma," she replied.

Thoughts of her quitting the club were beginning to surface. Where was her loyalty? She had so much to think about, then the phone rang. It was Candy.

"Girl, guess what I heard?!" she exclaimed eagerly, ready to spill some juice. "Last night your new boo got with Lil Secret and they went home together!" blurted out Candy.

"Oh my," Mya said, shocked. "You mean Lil Secret from our club?"

"Yes; she took him home, girl," answered Candy.

"Well, now, that confirms my decision to leave the club. How can your own club sister disrespect you in the blink of an eye?!" Mya exclaimed.

*'I'm done,'* she realized.

To top it all off, Lil Secret even called Mya to confirm the situation. It was a game to her; for Mya, it was not.

For some time, Mya stayed away from everyone on the motorcycle scene, with the exception of just a few people. One was Hollywood. Mya spent time with Candy at work then hung out with Candy's family in the evening at their mom's house, where all the children, grandchildren, and other friends came to be together. It didn't matter what was going on, they all stayed together like a big family, full of love and support.

P-Town reached out to Mya a few times, until finally he got her to meet him at a bar where he was shooting pool. He just smiled mostly. Mya thought something was wrong with how much he smiled with all his pretty gold fangs showing in his mouth. Every time anyone walked in or next to him, he greeted or hugged them. Everyone knew him, but Mya didn't know him that well.

"You thinking of riding a motorcycle?" he asked.

"Yeah, I want to soooo bad." She constantly pictured herself riding.

"You know you're welcome to join our club. I'm one of the founders," P-Town said, boasting.

Mya shrugged her shoulders. "Yeah, I think I would like to be in an all-women thing," she said softly.

"Cool; that's hot! You should definitely start a women's club, but y'all should be riding, not doing the social club thing. You want to ride, get all your girls and y'all ride. I can help you," he said proudly.

Mya got up from the chair and thought before she spoke. "I sure will think about it. I know my girl and her sisters will role with me," Mya said with confidence.

"Yeah, I saw y'all. I see you have a few people who have your back. You gon need it," P-Town insisted.

As Mya began to head out, P-Town dropped the pool stick and began to walk behind her.

"Call me," he said as he opened the door to let her out.

The next day, Mya began to talk with Candy, Hollywood, and a few of her other friends about starting a women's motorcycle club. They were all excited, but Mya was unsure that they could produce the bikes.

'It's gon be a long time before everyone has their own bike,' she thought.

# CHAPTER 5

After some time, Mya linked back up with P-Town and they began to talk more on starting the women's motorcycle club. P-Town and Mya began to work on colors and a centerpiece for the new club. They would name this club Ladies of Flavor. P-Town wanted to protect them, so he had Mya go from black vests to pink ones in order to be safer on the roads for the women. This also made them stand out.

Ladies of Flavor was beginning to become a reality. Candy was the first to buy her bike, and as each woman bought her bike, they asked P-Town to come along to help them purchase a good bike and to teach them how to ride.

By the end of the year, Mya had gotten together several women to participate. Candy, Charlie, Hollywood, DT, Lil D, Pebbles, Special K, and Baby Powder. All were African American, with different skin tones, body types, and faces, and all were not afraid to ride. They all liked challenges and they were ready to be loyal to their new sisters, but in Mya's mind, something was missing.

'If only we had a Puerto Rican, or a Spanish woman, and a white girl,' she thought, 'then Ladies of Flavor would really be everything the name says.'

P-Town pressured Mya so badly that she went to pick up her bike at the end of the fall. It was bright red, bigger than most sport bikes, and she had no idea what it was capable of doing. She just got it because P-Town insisted it was the bike for her.

"Besides, a president has to have a good bike and the toughest bike," he said with delight.

"So, what is it again?" Mya asked unsurely.

"It's a Busa, named after the fastest bird in China," P-Town said.

Mya shook her head. It all made sense to her now. She thought back to what Mr. Brown, her pops, had told her before he died. "You are an eagle!" And here it was, she would be riding a fast bird.

Mya began to smile and said, "Okay."

After they picked up the bike, Mya and P-Town stayed in the garage for hours just gazing over the bike. P-Town taught Mya the politics of the bike scene and warned her of her duties of being a president.

"You can't be all nice to your friends and let them get away with stuff. Y'all about to have a lot of females wanting to join. You will run them away if your friends get to do what they want and not participate like they should. You have to become a leader now, Mya. I name you myself: SUNRIZE!" P-Town said with full loyal confidence that it was the perfect name.

After they locked up the garage, P-Town followed Mya into her house.

"Where're you going?" she asked.

"With you," he smirked.

Mya headed upstairs to her bedroom and P-Town followed. And that was the beginning of P-Town and Mya's relationship.

The next day, they got up still talking about motorcycles and the club. P-Town reminded Mya about learning the bike and going to get her permit.

In the days to follow, P-Town and Mya were always together, talking and working on their main goal, Ladies of Flavor. She admired him a lot and their conversations were very intense.

"Y'all can come out now," P-Town informed Mya. "All of y'all will be riding by spring, and I've got your back. Y'all can let it be known at our dance this Halloween," P-Town announced. "All of our chapters will be there, and I'll make sure your club is protected."

Now, see, when you say protected in the bike scene that means, when a club comes in, they should go to the heads first. The heads are the elders who say if it's okay for you to start a club, but P-Town thought, since he was considered the head of his own club and had chartered other clubs, that if the Ladies of Flavor ran under them, they wouldn't have any problems. Mya believed in P-Town, but she knew this was going to be a challenge.

She simply replied, "Okay, P. We'll be ready."

Mya set up a meeting to talk with the women in her new club. All of them were tough in their own way. Candy was quiet but kept a pistol somewhere. She really wasn't into the whole thing, but she wanted to protect Mya from others who meant her no good. Charlie was an old friend Mya had met years back and they'd hung out on the rough sides of town together. Hollywood was from her old club, the Choir Angels, and loved the bike scene the most. She definitely was ready to ride.

Pebbles was Candy's baby sister who'd only come in to make sure things stayed regulated. Lil D was Mya's buddy from her part-time job who believed that whatever Mya said could be done. DT was an older woman who loved young men, but she was a fighter. She was voted immediately as the sergeant-at-arms. Baby Powder was the youngest and they'd given her the name because she was a plus-size girl who had the cutest dimples and smile and she talked so soft.

Mya's first assessment was to have them watch a video of women brawling. Of course, DT, Pebbles, and Mya were excited by the shouting and acted like they were dabbing at each other. The rest stayed quiet, except for Baby Powder, who put her hands over her face, asking everyone to let her know when it was over.

Mya laughed to herself as she looked upon them. "This is my club!"

P-Town came into the house and began laughing and socializing with the other ladies. "Y'all ready?" he asked?

DT was the first to say something. "Yeah, bro; we 'bout that life!" she answered.

He looked down at the TV and cut his eyes at Mya. "Really?" He chuckled.

Mya nodded her head yes. In her mind, she said, *'I have to know who I've got to watch out for.'*

The night of P-Town's club's annual dance arrived. All the women had showed up just like when Mya was with Bambi and all the ladies had showed up to participate. Mya had learned some important things from Bambi, so this time, it was with a twist: Candy with the pistol packed to her side, and Mya with four knives packed all over her. DT with a hammer and screwdriver; Pebbles with about fourteen weapons in her purse, which she'd used way before they'd formed a club. They were ready to protect who they were. They were ready to be respected as women on bikes; they were ready for any challenge.

Mya texted P-Town to let him know they were on their way in, and just like P-Town had told her, his members were waiting and securing the area when the ladies walked in. There were one-two-three-four-five-six-seven-eight ladies in pink vests besides Mya! This was something that hadn't been done before, so the look on most faces was shock, misunderstanding, anger, and wtf. Some were happy to see Mya and the ladies, some were not, but most of all, they were showed love by P-Town's club and given respect and introduced to the motorcycle scene.

Wherever Mya walked, the club walked too. If they didn't, the sergeant-at-arms was there and the rest made sure they stayed together, waiting patiently for their president.

Before the night ended, a trophy count came about. This was for the ones who'd participated in colors to win a trophy for their club based off how many attended. They had the most in attendance, most out of state, most in a social club, most in motor sport, and the most ladies in attendance. And there it was: Ladies of Flavor, first night out, got the trophy for Ladies MC in attendance. Everyone was in shock. The look on the faces of some of the people was astonishment. Ladies of Flavor was overexcited. They had come to enter this world, not knowing they would be leaving with a trophy.

P-Town nodded at Mya from a distance. She nodded back, saying thank you. After that, many other clubs walked up, showing them love and wanting to introduce themselves. It was official, Ladies of Flavor had been put on the map.

৯◆৶

The task wasn't easy keeping the women together and available to participate, but Mya would always help with rides, babysitting when needed since she had an older child who would watch the little ones, and she helped make sure some of them had money for the events as well. P-Town stayed on top of Mya about her presidential duties, such as: Never talk to a man on the set for more than four minutes; watch all of your vests; and, don't be too friendly, letting just anyone approach you. The last one was hard for Mya because she was very friendly and flirtatious, but P-Town insisted that would be her downfall if she didn't listen.

"Teach your girls the same," he instructed.

By spring, P-Town was ready to pull Mya's bike out to help her learn how to ride. He first taught her on his bike, which was an 1100 Yamaha. Mya had a 1300 Hayabusa and P-Town didn't want her to scratch it up learning, so he insisted she ride his.

He began to teach Mya with himself on one side of her and his brother Nate on the other side. He had already taught Mya the fundamentals while she was testing for her permit, so getting on it and riding in first gear would be her first lesson. Mya had all the gear on from boots to knee pads to a fully padded motorcycle jacket and helmet. P-Town rarely wore a helmet, but he was an excellent coach. She hopped on, seemingly with much confidence, but deep down, she was scared to death. When P-Town instructed her to turn on the motorcycle, she was terrified.

P-Town hollered at her, "YOU GOTTA DO THIS! NO TURNING BACK!"

Mya turned the bike on, gripped the handles, and put the gear in first. Letting go of the clutch and turning the handle for gas, the bike began to move slowly—Mya was riding! It wasn't like it had been when she'd rode on the back of Racer's bike. This was different. She couldn't enjoy the ride or find peace because she had to concentrate on the bike. Even though her stomach was in knots, she had a big Kool-Aid grin on her face, but as she came to a stop, she tipped over. She didn't put her feet down. P-Town came right away and picked her up.

"You've got no choice but to get back on," he said.

As they made it to the end of the ride, Candy was there waiting and sitting on her bike. She'd gone to bike school to learn and hadn't gotten the hands-on, back-road, rough-neck treatment Mya was getting, but Candy was a diva and they all learned different. It didn't bother Mya because she wanted what was best for each of them.

Then Special K came with her guy Lil Dip. She also had been to bike school and rode a cruiser. Mya liked to learn from the streets and learn from a president who could teach her the real, for deep inside, she needed to be better than the rest of them. They lined the women up and followed close behind. They rode many of the back roads, county lines, and short dead ends until P-Town felt Mya had gotten it down pat. After their first lesson, both Candy and Special K felt they didn't need to be escorted home, but Mya insisted they trail them home.

By the next lesson, Special K felt she was ready. "I already know how because I got my training through the class," she bragged. She then told them she would meet them.

Mya and P-Town snapped at her, but she wouldn't listen. She took off on her bike anyway, with her guy following her. Minutes later, Mya got a call that Special K was down. Mya and P-Town rushed to the scene only to see Special K with her foot dangling from her leg at the ankle bone. She had caught it between her bike and the curb while making a wide turn and had fallen over. Mya immediately parked the best she could and ran over to Special K's side. Lil Dip was there, calling the ambulance.

When Mya approached Special K, she could see how the foot was detached and broken off from the bone; the skin was all that was keeping it together.

"Oh, sis, why're you so hardheaded?" Mya asked, disappointed.

"I'm sorry, little sister; I was trying to make you proud of me," Special K said sadly, in pain.

Mya stood up to keep from crying and called all the members to let them know Special K was down, meaning she had fallen on her bike. Those who could make it showed up at the hospital and stayed until Special K had surgery. Special K was down as a rider and Mya supported her with whatever she needed.

"It's hard like that sometimes," instructed P-Town, "but you still have to keep the club going. Don't lose sight of it now."

In two weeks, Mya was riding with P-Town everywhere. She even rode with him when he rode with his club. They took her on fast runs, and the police even stopped them from time-to-time because of the fast speeds.

It was important that riders get their motorcycle license. Some men who rode with them were missing either their driver's license or their motorcycle license. Mya made a note to add that as a requirement in her bylaws for Ladies of Flavor. She had witnessed so many times with the men how the police would pull them over and find that some of them were without license. Bikers never leave each other alone, but when something like that happened, they had to improvise with the situation.

P-Town and Mya became inseparable. They spent long hours doing club stuff and riding; then, when they were done, they shared the same bed. To everyone else, she was his woman. To Mya, they were just good friends because P-Town had never really made it clear they were a couple. He'd just said he wasn't seeing anyone.

One day while riding with P-Town's club, a white girl came with her mixed brother who was super fine. She and Mya hit it off well and decided to ride beside each other behind P-Town. Every move he made, they made; every turn he made, they made just like him with perfection.

"I like her," Mya said to herself.

They stopped to eat and take a break, and that's when she greeted Mya. "I'm Beth."

Mya said, "I'm Sunrize."

"I like riding with you," Beth said with enthusiasm. "When can we do this again?"

Mya was thrilled. "When are you free?"

"Like whenever."

Mya was very happy; the pieces were falling together. She'd finally gotten another race in the club, just like the centerpiece she'd had made with a black, white, and brown-skinned girl on the back. She looked over at P-Town, and just like they always did, they nodded at each other.

After they finished eating, they all lined up again and raced back into the city on the expressway with

Mya and Beth staying together in harmony. This time they were nodding at each other, letting the other know what they were about to do. They had bonded.

# CHAPTER 6

It was the beginning of summer and time for a monthly meeting. Some of the women hadn't been attending or participating in the scheduled events, including Candy. Mya was beginning to feel the need to let some of them go. As the meeting began, they heard a bike pull up. It was Beth. She got off the bike in a hurry to be a part of Mya and the other ladies. Beth was a nice-looking woman. She was a lot like Mya with a tomboy attitude; she liked to fix things, loved to work on bikes. She carried a pistol too, but on the bike.

It was a shock to the other women because she was white, but to Mya, it was exactly what the club needed. The look on Mya's face made the other women change their demeanor and welcome Beth right in. Mya named her Isis. Beth became the road captain as she had the most experience in riding. The group was coming together. Now all they had to do was get rid of the ones who were lagging behind.

The first to go was Baby Powder. She'd always had an issue with Mya, so Mya hadn't put much faith in her membership from the beginning. There was talk about Charlie leaving, but Mya wasn't ready to part with her yet and tried to work with her on her attendance.

Hollywood had gotten with Racer, who had gone to be president of another club. She hadn't left

Ladies of Flavor yet, but she so wanted to be with her mate, and by rights, there was nothing wrong with that. So, she took some time away to decide what she wanted to do. By the end of the year, a younger version of Mya had come along—Baby B. She wanted to ride, she wanted to participate, and Mya asked P-Town to help her with getting a bike and learning to ride it. Her bike was green, her helmet was a Mohawk, and she was very petite and neat. Mya knew she would be a great fit.

The bike season ended with Mya, Isis, and Baby B doing most of the riding. They could hardly ever get Candy to ride with them, and when she did, she wouldn't hang or ride as much as they were use to doing. The rest of the girls would show up in their cars and follow behind them. They only wanted to get to whatever spot and drink. Baby B would always pressure Mya about how the rest of them weren't riding and how maybe they needed to be suspended.

"I'm telling you, Sunrize, this ain't fair!" she snapped.

"I understand, but right now, let's try to grow the club with the ones who are down, and let the ones who aren't fall to the wayside," Mya rationalized.

Baby B believed in Ladies of Flavor. She could see how much potential the club had. She helped plan events for the dances and cookouts, went to many events with sometimes just her and Mya; she was a very strong member. Isis, Baby B, and Mya rode the city and attended events everywhere. They even planned a trip to Myrtle Beach for bike week.

The trip to Myrtle Beach forged a bond that Baby B, Isis, and Mya would never forget. The long ride through the night got them there, where they bunked with a few riders from another club whose president Mya knew. She asked them to make room for the women.

The first morning, they took off to see the sites and meet other bikers. On each block, a biker club was hosting something. Some were barbequing, some were frying fish, and some were making pots—BIG pots—of gumbo. They were friendly to one another and made sure to ask if anyone was hungry. They did line dances right in the street, across from the beach. Every room on the beach belonged to a biker club and every room was open to everyone. Food, drinks, and hospitality were the subject.

Isis was into bike stunts, so she made sure they attended the stunt sessions. Mya was into the paint jobs and cool bikes. She even had a little done to her bike as well. She even found a knife shop which had the coolest knives and swords she had ever seen. But something was missing. Enjoying all the fun and the beach made them miss their co-members they'd left behind, wishing they all would have come

"See, Sunrize, if the club would learn to participate more, we would be so great," Baby B blurted out with a sad look on her face.

Their time of enjoying bike week was over and they all were ready to get back home. On the way home, Mya began feeling sick and asked to pull over a lot more than usual. She even threw up a few times along the way.

"Wow, Sunrize, are you okay?" Isis asked surprisingly. "You sure a baby isn't in there?" she asked sarcastically as Baby B chuckled.

"Funny, funny, funny" Mya snapped, but deep inside, she knew she just might be pregnant. She was glad when they pulled the bikes so she could sleep. That was how those three were: they looked out for each other in a manner that showed they were one.

When they returned, they had to stop at their set to handle a couple of loose things, one pertaining to a member whose colors they needed to get. It was funny like that in a bike club. A woman never really had time for a lot of other lady-like things, such as her first stop should have been home to check in with her children.

The member had violated and stayed drunk, not listening to any of the other members. She'd put her club in a bad situation by fighting and cursing at them. That was a NO-NO to Mya. She'd even put that in her newly-issued club rules. It was Claire; she was so pissed at Baby B for leaving her, she'd started up a lot of confusion. Candy and the others couldn't handle the situation, so they'd waited patiently for the president to return.

As Mya, Isis, and Baby B entered the club, a man bumped into Mya and said, "Excuse me. You are beautiful!" he gawked, but Mya was focused on the situation she was about to engage in. "Look, my name is Manny. I really would like to get to know you."

"Right now is not a good time," Mya murmured. "I've got club stuff right now; can I get back with you?"

"Okay; I'll be at the end table by the bar," he answered.

As Mya walked up to the club members, Claire was sitting there, still mad. "What's your problem?" Mya asked.

Claire stood there silently and wouldn't respond. She stared at Baby B as if she wanted to fight her.

"Look, if you have an issue, you need to address your problem with me!" Mya exclaimed.

Claire picked up her glass and followed Mya outside. "Sunrize, you're good people; it doesn't have anything to do with you. I can't believe how Baby B got into this and changed; she forgot all about me!" Claire cried out.

"She is participating, and that's a lot more than I can say about the other members," Mya remarked.

"See, the thing is, this isn't for everyone. Either you feel it and it becomes a part of you, or you don't. You need to decide if this is for you. You can't be mad because she wants to participate and enjoy her members," she said with authority.

Claire drank from her cup and began to remove her vest. Mya was crushed but kept a straight face. She knew if this woman was ready to go, she couldn't plead for her to stay. There only would be more problems along the way.

"Sunrize," said Claire, "you are a wonderful person and you don't judge people—that's why I came in—but this isn't for me."

Mya nodded her head in acceptance and politely took the vest from Claire. "Okay."

From that point, there was no more talking. Claire removed herself from the parking lot and rode away. The others began to come outside to see if it was safe and to check on their president. She turned and said, "Everything's fine."

Another person waiting was Manny. He was watching from a distance, making sure Mya was okay. He waved at her to let her know he was watching.

She walked over to him and said, "I'm sorry you had to witness our mess," she said calmly.

"No, I'm fine, just making sure you're okay," he replied. "What's your name?"

"Sunrize," she answered.

"No; I mean your real name."

"Why?"

"Because I really would like to get to know you," he replied with confidence.

"Look, dude, I'm pregnant! That's my name!" she snapped and started to walk off.

"So WHAT?" he yelled. "I know you feel the chemistry. Can I at least can give you my number?"

Mya took Manny's number and continued walking away.

ชั่ ◆ ชั่

P-Town's bike was down due to an engine issue and he began asking Mya if he could ride her bike. This began to take a toll on her as she often wanted to get out and ride herself, but sometimes, when she came home, he would have hopped on it and was gone.

"This isn't going to work," she uttered.

Baby B had pulled up, thinking they were about to ride, when she looked in the already-opened garage and saw that P-Town had taken Mya's bike. Once she parked, she started right in on Mya.

"SEE, SUNRIZE, THIS ISN'T COOL. DOESN'T HE REALIZE YOU ARE SOMEONE'S PRESIDENT?" she shouted. "THIS ISN'T RIGHT!" she repeated.

Just as they began to let the garage door down, they heard a bike. It was P-Town. As he pulled up, there was some scratches on the side of the fender. Baby B shook her head in disbelief. P-Town parked and got off with a messed-up look on his face.

"Yeah, I let dude ride it and he's gon fix it," he uttered quickly.

"What?!" Mya snapped.

"Yeah, he paints bikes, so he said let him ride it, and if he messed it up, he would re-paint it," P-Town said sarcastically.

"Why would you do that? It isn't yours to allow someone else to ride it?!"

"I JUST SAID IT'S 'BOUT TO LOOK BETTER THAN BEFORE!"

Baby B put her head down and almost cried. "He just killed your season!" she said with disgust.

Mya walked away, disappointed. Just as she thought she could trust P-Town, he'd gone and showed her his ugly.

The next day, Mya took a pregnancy test to confirm what she already knew then called P-Town. His reaction to her pregnancy hurt, the infamous question a lot of men ask.

"Is it mine?" he blurted out.

Which sent Mya into a whirlwind. She backed away from him and limited the places she went on the bike scene to avoid seeing him, but she kept in touch about the updates on her bike being repainted.

*Months Later ~*

As Mya began to show with her pregnancy, she started experiencing member concerns in the club. Who was gonna step up while Sunrize was out, they all wondered and talked among themselves. That was hard for Mya because all of them were great and she loved each and every one of them, but none of them could possibly be the person she needed them to be to keep the club together and going.

She wanted to look to P-Town for that answer, but with the new baby coming, their relationship was rocky. P-Town had been lying about being with another woman—possibly *two* other women—and Mya was trying to keep calm and say nothing to him. She put him in the category with the rest of the men who had hardened her heart. She had started spending time with Manny—who spoiled her by catering to her every craving—since she knew P-Town was uninterested and would choose anything the bike life was doing over her and the baby. He still was a leader and a founder of a club she respected, so she called him for an answer. His answer wasn't what she had expected.

"Ms. Outgoing. Why?"

"Well, she is a business-savvy person and doesn't mess with anyone on the bike scene. The influences of a man will mess y'all's club up," he said harshly.

Mya got right off the phone and called for a meeting.

The next day at the meeting, Mya looked at all of her flavors, her members, her sisters, then began to speak.

"Well, I know you all know I need to take some time away and I need to appoint someone to be in charge in my absence. Ms. Outgoing will step up as vice president and will be your go-to person until I am able to come back."

Some of the members were very upset. Some felt they should have had that spot, and the one she'd thought would ride it out was especially upset. It was Baby B. Baby B began to shy away from Mya at the events, making sure she showed up late and unbothered. There were others who began to talk of leaving, but all Mya could do now was concentrate on having the baby.

Ms. Outgoing threw Mya a baby shower, but a lot of members were still upset, so only Isis, Candy, Special K, Lil D, and the new member Spicy, who was Puerto Rican, showed up to the clubhouse for the baby shower outside of Candy's sisters, who were Mya's play big sisters.

Hollywood, Mya's favorite biker sister, showed up and showed much love for her sister. Every time one of them was going through something, the other would come just in time to show her support.

"You know I'm always gon be here, Sunrize," Hollywood whispered in Mya's ear as she hugged her.

The moment Mya heard that, she felt like everything else was nothing. It was like that between the two of them. No one else could understand.

In the shadow of it all sat Manny, making sure Mya was okay from a distance. He'd fallen in love with her power and her courage to endure the pain she was going through. But as Mya looked at him, she couldn't help thinking, '*This dude is not on the scene. What should I do?*' she thought.

She approached him and asked, "So what do you really want with me? I'm a biker chick, not your kind of daily woman!"

"I want you to be okay," said Manny. "I want you."

"You know I come with crazy people, and I'm not gon change my bike life," she said boastfully.

"I'm okay with that, sweetheart; just be true to me," he replied.

Mya's smile was huge and she began to walk back over to her event.

While they were talking, Hollywood was watching Manny and Mya's body language. "Who is that?" she asked when Mya came back over to where she was sitting.

"Sis, that's my friend. He's good," said Mya.

"Okay; I don't wanna have to call for reinforcements!" Hollywood stated.

As the days passed on, the members who had a problem with the club began to become more distant, while others began to come in. Mya didn't want any new members until she was able to really examine them, watch over them, and check them out.

The day the baby came home, the members begin turning in their colors. Surprised by it all, Ms. Outgoing came in to turn in her colors along with the Puerto Rican chick Spicy. Mya was hurt, but her goal was to get healed. With the baby on her shoulder, she accepted their colors without warrant and moved on.

Candy met with Baby B to turn in her colors, because she knew this one out of them all would hurt Mya the most. Candy kept Baby B's colors and never brought them to Mya. She knew how she felt about Baby B.

P-Town tried to become part of the baby and Mya's life, and he began to try to stay over more to help out with the baby at night. But for Mya, it was over between her and P-Town. She knew she was nothing more to him than something to play with. Mya wanted more, as she had always wanted more.

"How much am I worth if his focus is on everything else?" she asked herself.

She received a call that her bike was ready. Mya called Isis, as Isis was the best one to examine a bike. She still was the road captain and her bond with Mya hadn't changed. When they arrived to pick the bike up, they noticed there wasn't one bike painted red or one with any red on it.

An Asian man approached them and said, "I'm Rick. Are you Sunrize?"

"Yes," Mya said firmly as she looked over to Isis.

"Well, here's your baby."

They looked over at a bike which had a green tint to it, but as they looked around it, it flipped colors.

"THIS IS NOT WHAT I WANTED!" she yelled. "P-Town said you would put it back to its original color but better. This is not red!" she stated.

"I'm sorry, but he specifically picked this color, or wet, for you," he said with confidence.

"Oh, man, this is not lady-like!" she snapped.

"Well, I can keep it and change it, but it may take some time," he said.

"No; no more keeping my bike. It's almost riding season!"

# CHAPTER 7

About six months had passed and Mya had begun working on the club and meeting with her members on how the club was going. Putting the club back on its feet was a task. She had to get back out on the scene and fly colors, attending events and other set nights regularly by herself mostly, which took about four nights a week, to let the MC scene know the Ladies of Flavor weren't going anywhere.

Ms. Outgoing and Spicy had joined another club called Speed Ways, and Baby B had become vice president of a motor sports club called Headlines. When Mya would see them, she gave them the same respect she gave to anyone else.

Isis and Mya stayed on the bikes and ran them hard, stopping and speaking to all their biker friends and family. A lot of people tripped out on Mya's new paint job and how they knew P-Town had had something to do with it, so she made sure she kept adding features to it. She had it stretched out and bought new chrome rims with matching chrome handle grips.

At this time, it was getting difficult for Isis as she needed a babysitter a lot, so Mya found others to ride with when Isis couldn't. Manny would call and ask if she needed anything, if she'd had a good day, how was the baby—all the things Mya wanted a man to ask her. Been here before, she told herself, but this time I'm gonna do the opposite. Mya stopped seeing P-Town... and began seeing Manny.

P-Town was not happy with her new relationship with Manny, so he continued to be a thorn in her side, except on the motorcycle scene. When she was there, he would send his members over to make sure she was okay. He would watch her back constantly to make sure no other man was trying to push up on her. But reality was that Mya, his Sunrize, had moved on and just wanted to make sure she was respected as a biker. When they weren't on the motorcycle scene, he gave them problems. He would show up unannounced, call or prank call them anonymously, harass Mya about the baby, and most of all, try to dictate to her when she was out with Manny.

Manny showered Mya with gifts and clothes, and gave the girls the attention they needed, especially when Mya was out on the scene. He made sure she was happy—until a few of his coworkers started to enlighten him on what they thought a biker chick was and what she was possibly doing on the bike scene.

"I couldn't be committed to one of those!" the first coworker said.

"Yeah; you don't know who she's fucking!" said the second coworker.

Manny started to apply pressure to Mya about her whereabouts and her history with P-Town. It didn't matter how much she tried to make Manny feel secure, it was embedded in him that a biker girl was a whore, so they began to fight and argue, with Manny saying sarcastic things about Mya's bike life every time. The crazy part was he wouldn't leave her alone, but continued to show her how insecure he was about it.

Mya figured moving might help relieve Manny of his feelings of thinking P-Town knew too much about her, so Mya and Manny moved in together in a new apartment. Manny was upset during the process. He had just lost his grandmother, the woman who'd raised him, and was drinking uncontrollably. Mya felt she could handle it; she had so many sisters and brothers on the bike scene who had been through or were going through something similar. She was understanding and made no comments to hurt him.

A few months after, it was a cold winter and Valentine's Day had come. Mya just knew Manny would shower her with gifts, but he told her he didn't celebrate Valentine's Day, so Mya and Hollywood went shopping and bought gifts for themselves— perfume, outfits, and shoes—things that make a woman happy! Enthused about the dance the new club Hollywood was joining was having that night, they were full of joy and ready to party and have fun.

That night, Mya and her club sisters attended Hollywood's bike club's dance and tried to enjoy their night with her. They began to dance and drink and mingle with their sisters and brothers. Baby B saw Mya and even joined her on the dance floor. After the dance, they decided to go to an after set. Candy didn't go, but asked the new sergeant-at-arms, Ms. Pie, if Mya would be okay. Ms. Pie replied, "I've got her!" Candy departed the scene.

At the after set, Mya joined a few more of her biker sisters and ate and drank some more. "I think I've had enough," she said to Baby B, who was there among the crowd. Ms. Pie was entertaining a man and wasn't paying any attention to Mya, her president, so Baby B walked over and tapped her on the shoulder.

"Sunrize is ready to go."

Ms. Pie was very upset, but murmured, "Okay."

When they got in the car, Ms. Pie said, "Drop me off up the street, Sunrize."

Intoxicated but feeling alert, Mya agreed. Mya rode up the street and dropped Ms. Pie off.

On the way home, Mya began to listen to a song which touched her heart about what was going on in her life. She had lost many members; now Hollywood was leaving, and neither Candy nor Isis was participating much, Manny hadn't got her anything for Valentine's Day, and she even thought a little bit about her career. She felt like she didn't want to exist any more and wished she could just disappear.

In her feelings, Mya fell asleep at the wheel. In her sleep, she saw people in white all around her, hovering over her body. Then, out of nowhere, she saw her daddy, Mr. Brown. He touched her shoulder and said, "You can go now!" Mya jumped up, not realizing she was stuck and why.

When Mya awoke, she was covered by her airbag and tried to reach to open her door. Someone came to her window and said, "Don't move!" It was a man who must have witnessed what had just happened. Finally, the fire department came and got Mya out of the car, laying her body on the stretcher. One fireman whispered to the other, "Her legs are broken." Mya began to understand that something bad has happened. Then she felt the pain and screamed!

The ambulance rushed her to the hospital as a police officer rode in the back with Mya and asked her many questions, but she couldn't reply. All she heard when she tried to speak was static and nothing came out. She was taken straight into the Trauma Unit of the Emergency Room. The nurses on the unit came to her and asked her could she give them a number to call family. She shook her head no. Another nurse attempted to have Mya spell it out. Mya began to think of her mother and remembered her mom's house phone. "5... 5... 5... 6... 8... 8... 1... 2... 3... 4..." The nurse rushed to call the number.

Once the hospital got Mya stabilized, people began to enter. Mya saw people come in and out, lying on her bed; sometimes there were ten people in the room at a time—all of her family and her extended families. Her kids, her cousins, her play sisters, and her biker family. She was in so much pain that she remained quiet, trying to let the morphine take effect. Then she began to look for Manny, wondering to herself where was he.

Ms. Pie came in with Isis and Hollywood, and began to cry with them, holding hands. Mya nodded her head and looked over to her cousin Brenda as she knew Ms. Pie was not valid. Baby B came in and got in the bed with Mya, and her biker brother Z-Man sat at the foot. Z-Man had been Mya's big brother on the scene for a very long time and kicked his duties in when needed.

The doctor came in and told them he would have to operate quickly as she was suffering from a femur fracture, had had a light stroke, and had some broken ribs. As the transporters came in to move Mya, Manny walked in, with P-Town not far behind. Manny kissed Mya on top of her head as the transporters rolled her away with P-Town holding the baby and watching them.

"I tell you what it was," people began to ramble in the waiting room.

"They said she hit a city bus!" someone chatted.

"And she was drunk!" another one added on.

But Mya's closest people just stayed quiet. There were so many bikers there that they had no room to sit. Someone ordered pizzas to keep everyone calm while they awaited the outcome of Mya's surgery. To the bikers, it was Sunrize, their sister, and they all were concerned. To some people, she was at the end, and they couldn't see her being able to come out of this one at all. Mrs. Brown showed up and asked the hospital to get rid of all the people. Many did it out of respect, if that was her wish, but would later tell Mya they had been upset.

When Mya woke up and was back in her room, hooked up to a machine which she could press the button to administer her pain medicine, she noticed her leg was fully bandaged and underneath were staples. She couldn't move that well and she felt very weak.

A couple of days later, a nurse came in and told her, in order to leave the ICU, she had to be able to get up, and as bad as it hurt, attempt to stand. Mya pushed herself with the help of a nurse assistant and stood up. Even though that was step one for the hospital, it was her first step to fighting with all her might to begin to beat all the odds—which she seemed to have done time-and-time again.

A week later, in her new room, Mya wasn't able to get up without help and had to learn through physical therapy how to walk all over again. Ms. Brown made it so that Mya's room number wasn't posted so she could limit how many people could visit Mya until she was feeling better. Every day, she met with a physical therapist, an occupational therapist, and a speech therapist because the hospital had determined that Mya hadn't been able to speak in the ambulance because she'd had a stroke.

One day, a very tall and large woman entered the room and woke her up for a bath. Mya had never been in a situation where someone else had to wash her up or bathe her. The thought of having someone see her body drove her insane.

"Don't worry, Miss; you'll be fine once you're all cleaned up," the woman said.

For four weeks Mya remained in the hospital dealing with the fact that she couldn't do much of anything. She sometimes daydreamed about the day she would appear on a white horse—not sure why she kept seeing a white horse instead of her motorcycle—but she smiled at the thought anyway.

Manny walked in one day with a surprise. He had found her phone in her totaled car, and although it was a little damaged, she could retrieve her contacts. He also brought the girls to see Mya. She'd missed them so much. All she could do was smile because she didn't want them to know she was hurting and depressed. Just seeing the little one, who had just turned one year old, helped her to find the strength to challenge herself every day to get better. When the baby got up and walked, Mya could not believe it.

"She's walking!" she exclaimed.

Everyone in the room was happy, and Mya was content now and could rest for the day.

On the outside, there were problems with the club. Candy was trying to keep order for her, but no one would listen. Ms. Pie was trying to quit and her reason was, since there was no Sunrize riding right now, the club would fall.

"So you gon bail out now when she needs you?" asked Candy.

Ms. Pie nodded and said she would give it a few more weeks. Isis was worried about Sunrize's health and cared less if she would ride again. She knew she was loyal and just wished all the fakers would leave. There was a war between those who felt the club was gone and those who would rise to keep it together.

Then, one day, a friend of Candy's came to visit her; her name was Deranged. She spoke of joining the club and bringing in maybe two more people. Deranged was a big, beautiful Amazon. She was high-yellow, six-three, and everything on her body was proportioned. She was definitely a queen and fit Ladies of Flavor. All Mya could do was put a pleased expression on her face because she knew a person like her wouldn't fold, and with everything going on, she was ready to come in and see Flavor get to the next level.

The day came when Mya, Miss Sunrize, could go home. She agreed to schedule therapies because she still was not able to walk and was confined to a wheelchair until the stitches came out. Manny, however, was dealing with his own issues of being able to take care of her while she was in this condition.

"I was supposed to walk away," he said, "but my heart is too big. My family says this isn't my problem, and I should sit back and let your family figure it out."

Mya dropped her head and said sincerely, "If you need to walk away, do what you gotta do."

Manny kept driving and said no more.

The road to recovery was rocky. Mya needed help getting in and out of bed, in and out of the tub. She used the walker to get around the apartment, and Manny would help her recline after she sat down. She was so depressed because she'd never thought she would end up like this; depending on someone else hurt the most. She had some type of therapy almost every day, and she also had to go to doctor appointments every other day to check her blood levels. The impact of the accident had made her recovery time very slow, and the stroke had caused her to be on blood thinners until they could operate to install a stent in her artery.

Mya began to be extremely frustrated and she began taking out her frustration on Manny. Sometimes, she would throw things at him, and other times, she would say things she didn't mean to get him to leave and stay gone for long hours. He contacted Candy and told her and the sisters that he was going crazy with Mya's attitude. They advised him that he should take a break and they would look in on her.

One issue Manny had going on was, prior to he and Mya moving in together, he'd had a relationship with a woman who'd gotten pregnant and was getting close to her delivery. The woman was nagging him about how he was with Mya when he should be with her. He also was dealing with the putdowns from his family and friends. Manny loved Mya and asked her to marry him while she was still in the wheelchair. Without any hesitation, Mya accepted the ring, but one thing still remained a factor in their relationship as Manny saw it: the baby-daddy from-hell he couldn't get rid of—Mr. P-Town.

Shortly after the break he was advised to take, Manny got the news that the baby was on its way. So, when he wasn't available for a few days, Mya called P-Town and told him in confidence what was going on. There was an annual dance in Illinois that P-Town and his club were going to attend. He asked Mya if she wanted to get out and go.

"I can pick you up. I wanted to ask you also if I could ride your bike as well," he murmured. "If I place you in the driver's seat, you should be able to drive my truck and follow me to the event."

When they arrived at the event, P-Town's members grabbed the door quickly to help Mya out. "Sunrize!" each one said as they greeted her with love. Mya had brought her crutches and they helped her get situated as she began to walk into the dance. Everyone stopped and greeted her; they were so happy to see her.

One biker even said, "I thought you were done!" he exclaimed.

Every move she made someone was there to help her, but even though everyone was excited to see her, inside Mya was very depressed. She tried to smile to fake it, but she knew she wasn't the same, and that pain, plus the pain she was having, made her miserable.

P-Town came over to her. "You're gonna be back to yourself soon," he assured her.

On the way home, as she followed P-Town riding her bike, she thought about her club and how much she missed all of them, even the ones who were no longer with them.

'We could have been something else—31 Flavors,' she reminisced.

Suddenly, P-Town pulled off at the exit and pulled up at a hotel. Then he approached the truck and said. "I know you aren't ready to go home."

Mya smirked at him, got out with the crutches, and began hopping toward the door of the hotel. Once in the room, they talked about the bike life and motorcycles all night. It was the deepest and best conversation they'd ever had, but Mya knew P-Town was the type of man who only enjoyed the bike life, and his thirst for so many women had taken him over. That was what was important to him.

'*I could never go back...*' she thought.

They fell asleep laughing as if they were best friends all over again.

The next day when Mya got home, P-Town was able to park Mya's bike back so Manny wouldn't notice it had been moved. She was surprised she hadn't heard a word from Manny.

'*I guess he's made a decision,*' she thought.

When the night came, Manny sent Mya a picture of the new baby with a message that said, *Be home soon.*

*A Month Later ~*

The club had a meeting to get the club up and moving again since they had been out of action since Mya's accident. Deranged and her mom, who used the name Bad Mamma-Jamma, had joined, and Ms. Pie was talking about leaving. Hollywood had waited patiently for her but went on to join the club her man was in. Mya wanted to give Ladies of Flavor a fight to stay in the game, but she needed women who understood, wouldn't quit, and would participate. Deranged's mother, Bad Mamma-Jamma, would be a very big piece of that beginning.

Photo day came and the women met with the photographer to begin working on their website. They all took pictures on their bikes, including Mya, who still couldn't walk but leaned up against her machine as if she could take off. Isis did get her on it and Mya was able to ride, but not so well yet. After talking to P-Town, he insisted she come with him and his club to motivate her to ride again and get better.

"Come on!" he exclaimed. "All you need to do is get out," he pressured.

As he pulled the bike out for Mya, she got on with no problem, but couldn't back it up with her legs because they were still quite weak.

"EVERY TIME YOU NEED TO PARK OR BACK UP, I'LL DO IT FOR YOU!" he yelled over the bikes revving up.

That day, Mya rode with P-Town and his members, and at each stop, they fellowshipped with the others and he parked her bike. Along the way, he bragged to their fellow riders that she had been in an accident, but she was back on and ready!

"Got more heart than most!" he said proudly.

Still the ride was different. Mya wasn't sure why, but she knew she was off some kind of way.

ও◆ও

A few months later, Mya was walking with only a cane and no longer needed the walker, crutches, or wheelchair. The club members gave her a pink cane to match her pink vest. Just when things were beginning to look up, Mya was shot down by Manny. He had been super nosy and had messed around and found the receipt from the hotel which matched the dates when he was gone for the birth of his baby.

"Wow, this was the same time my son was born, Mya!" he said as he put his head down.

"Oh, we stopped after the dance. I was really tired," she replied.

"Oh really?!" he snapped. "WHY HAVE PEOPLE BEEN TELLING ME THEY SEE A DUDE SOMETIMES RIDING YOUR BIKE?!" he yelled.

"I let P-Town ride it," she said, with no regard to his feelings as she drank from a water bottle. "You wouldn't understand. Even though he is my baby-daddy, he is a club founder and president. I let him ride it, damn it," she explained with no emotion. "It was important." Then she walked out the room.

"No, Mya, I'm done! I can't do this. I can't compete." Manny sighed.

Mya was sitting on the bed in the room, gazing off at the TV, acting as if she was ignoring him. Manny got dressed and left, and didn't return until the weekend was over. Mya, in a situation like that, always relied on her buddy Hollywood. No matter whether they were in the same club or not, she and Mya were close. Mya picked up the phone and vented to Hollywood the entire weekend Manny was gone.

"See, you know you're gonna have to fix it and do something with your baby-daddy, sister. He's gone and should be out the picture. Sunrize, fix it!" she snapped.

"I will, sister," Mya assured her.

But once Manny came home, she did the opposite. She acted as if nothing was wrong and continued to change nothing. No apology or security for Manny. She just got up and began to attend more biker events.

Through therapy, she began to lift her bike and park again without too many problems. By this time, Ms. Pie had left them and a new member, who was a Mexican, had joined and immediately became family. Her name was Grace. She was short, stocky, and full of humor, just what Mya needed as she kept Mya laughing and entertained.

New blood was beginning to start the new Flavor off, and even Desiree, Mya's daughter, who was now old enough to join, was beginning to attend events. Mya made sure Desiree had a bike and bought her a yellow CBR 929 Honda. P-Town was able to teach both Grace and Desiree at the same time. They named Desiree, PYT, a name fit for a princess. Grace had gone to motorcycle school, but P-Town taught her the fundamentals of being safe on the streets.

It had been some time since people had seen Ladies of Flavor riding together as a crew. Shortly after, they got word they had to attend a bike count to make sure enough of them were riding. Mya had gotten to know many of the leaders on the bike scene, and with no hesitation, she made sure to show up to any events that were about structuring the motorcycle scene. She was very open to it and never worried. One leader, G-Berry, came down from his chapter the weekend of the count to oversee Ladies of Flavor.

Although it was never easy getting all the Flavors together—sometimes it was impossible—but that day, they ALL showed up, riding one-by-one! Sunrize (Mya), Isis, Candy, Grace, PYT, and the non-riders who were in the process of getting their bikes, Deranged, Bad Mamma-Jamma, and Special K, an older woman who had been with them from earlier but who barely participated. She was great at cooking for the events they gave, but mostly, she believed in Mya.

After the count, most people stayed and hung out at one of the MC's club houses to socialize and drink. It was always a great feeling being around fellow bikers. Mya loved her brothers and sisters; it was a time to relax. G-Berry entertained the group of Flavors and offered them a drink he made called G-Berry juice, which consisted of moonshine, fruits, berries, and other things they didn't name. The girls were making faces because of the strong contents while some of the other bikers laughed.

The love in the building was unique, and as the time passed, the crowd began to fade, so the rest of the party decided to move the fun to a nearby local bar. There, they showed G-Berry a good time drinking, dancing, and talking mess, which was Bad Mamma-Jamma's favorite thing to do. Bad Mamma-Jamma was from Gary, Indiana, and she was at the age where she still claimed her set.

Bad Mamma-Jamma instantly became sergeant-at-arms as she watched over all the women in the club. At no time would she allow any of them to be alone. She loved men though and she loved to flirt. Her jokes sometimes hit below the belt of some of the men, but she didn't care. She was the spice Mya felt was needed for the club. She sat back and watched Bad Mamma-Jamma in disbelief, but finally, after a long time, she was satisfied with the mix of Flavor.

Back at home, things were beginning to take a spin. The mail had arrived and Manny had the results of a much-needed DNA test. It was conclusive: the baby wasn't his. Manny was sitting on the end of the bed when Mya came in from the bar. His face was full of guilt.

"I'm sorry, Mya. I really messed up and I've been acting real crazy. I've neglected you all this time, thinking I should have just been with her instead of you," he said sincerely.

Mya just smiled and said, "I'm about to take a bath."

During her bath, all she reflected on was her club. It was what made her the happiest. Her mind was relaxed, and thinking about what was going on with Manny was not important at this moment. The night ended in peace.

The next day, Mya walked into the garage and let the garage door up, when suddenly, PYT pulled up in her car, got out, and walked in the garage, straight over to her bike. Both of them began to gear up while their bikes were warming up. Then, as Mya pulled out, PYT followed. PYT was great at allowing her mother to lead. As they headed to the south side to meet Grace, they looked over at each other at times and just smiled. The ride was so peaceful.

Grace was always full of joy and laughed a lot with Mya, but one thing was for sure: her president was her total focus and she did her best to help enforce the rules Mya had put in place. She sometimes called Mya, "My precious Sunrize."

They met up at Grace's family's barbeque and met Grace's sisters, nephews, and nieces. Everyone there offered food and drinks, and they accepted Mya and PYT as family.

Mya texted Isis and Candy about riding, but they were always busy. It seemed hard just to get them all to meet up once a week to ride together. Things were always off for Mya. One would say Sunday, two would say on Monday, three on Saturday. Mya rode every day. By now, Mya had stretched and chromed out the Hayabusa and repainted it to where it flipped colors of purple, pink, and green. She loved it and had named her bike Betsy.

Grace and PYT were good riders and followed Mya well while riding, one reason Mya knew was because of their love of riding. Some of the other members had other reasons why they followed, and as time would come, they would eventually show her.

When the next club's dance came about, all of the Ladies of Flavor attended except Isis, who did not report her absence, and PYT, who'd gone out of town with her family. Mya, Deranged, Bad Mamma-Jamma, Candy, Pebbles, Grace, and a new member, Care Bear, were all in colors. They'd brought some extra people with them. Candy and Pebbles had brought their older sister, Tammy Lynn, and Mya had brought her friend Kelly, who was a white girl she knew from riding. Mya called her Farrah Faucet and hoped the crew would bond with her as someone of interest to join the club. Who also had come to support his woman was Manny.

Before the night got started good, as soon as Mya turned her head and begin to entertain her company, Bad Mamma-Jamma had an argument with another woman from Da Pits Motorsport Club.

"Sorry, Farrah; let me get over there."

Mya dashed over to the crowd of brawling women to break it up. When she approached Bad Mamma-Jamma, she asked, "What's going on?"

"Ain't nobody talkin' to dis heifer and she started talkin' shit!" Bad Mamma-Jamma replied loudly, one hand pointing and the other on her hip.

Bad Mamma-Jamma was no punk by far. Most times, she threw up her set with her hands, which Mya never really understood, but she knew Bad Mamma-Jamma definitely had a criminal life and possibly a gang life in another life.

"Okay! Calm down! No drama! Leave it alone, Mamma!" Mya snapped.

She stepped back over toward Farrah to finish their conversation, when suddenly, Bad Mamma-Jamma was walking back toward the woman she'd had words with and began to speak. In an instant, she had grabbed the woman and the floor went wild. Mya could barely see her club, nothing but pink stood out, and she began to go back in. She saw Deranged throwing females, Pebbles kicking them once they hit the floor, their sister Tammy Lynn on top of the bar throwing bottles and beer, Candy dead smack in the middle alongside Care Bear trying to make peace, and poor Grace asking for help.

Mya was heated, and as she entered into the middle, she felt a tug on her belt. It was Manny pulling at the belt on her pants.

"NOOOOOO, WOMAN! YOU'VE GOT TOO MANY HEALTH ISSUES!" he hollered.

She turned to him and said, "Those are my sisters!"

He grabbed her, spun her around, and jumped in and helped separate them to keep her out of it. As the crowd began to clear, they counted everyone up in the club, but then Deranged realized she didn't see her mother. Security and other bikers began to put them all out except Mya. No one ever touched her because she was their founder/president. In fact, the other leaders asked her to stay back for safety precautions, but her sergeant-at-arms, Bad Mamma-Jamma, was missing.

Manny stood by the door on the outside, worried that someone was gonna hurt Mya, but she came to the door unharmed.

"Everything is okay," she said as she stepped out the door.

At the bottom of the steps was Bad Mamma-Jamma. Mya looked at her, and for the first time, she was without her security and her club had been clowned.

"What happened?" she asked, disappointed. No one responded. "Okay, let's go home!" Mya demanded.

Manny ran and grabbed the car, then suddenly, Mya's phone rang; it was P-Town.

"What's up? Y'all good? We're on our way!" he exclaimed.

"No, P! We've got it under control. We're leaving now!" Then she hung up.

No matter what, P-Town was always going to come help Ladies of Flavor, but Mya felt, as the president, she could handle the situation. When she got in the car, she became silent and said no more.

Manny grabbed her and began to snap. "Maaan, Bad Mamma-Jamma's gonna get somebody hurt!" he exclaimed. "I told them, let something happen to my baby if y'all want to!" he clicked.

That was the first time Manny and Mya had been out as a couple on the bike scene, and after that, she thought he probably wouldn't try to come again. As far as Farrah, well, she knew there was too much going on, and the crew had pretty much showed her a little too much that night, but Mya was always hopeful.

A few days went by and the club assembled for a meeting.

"You guys, what happened out there?" Mya asked with concern.

Everyone began telling a portion of the story and she got a clear picture of how it had started. PYT attended the meeting. She had been absent for the dance due to family obligations on her father's side. Isis again was a no-show.

"Bad Mamma-Jamma, I told you to let it go. How do you go from letting it go to fighting after I clearly gave an order?"

Bad Mamma-Jamma hadn't said anything. Then she replied with guilt, "They grabbed me and put something over my head! Next thing I know, I was outside," she said in disbelief. "I'm sorry, daughter!" she said with sadness.

Mya pondered over the whole ordeal in silence. "Y'all don't listen," she said in a quiet voice. "Why should we carry on? I have done everything in my power to keep us all together," she said with disappointment.

Deranged watched Mya and her body language. She knew deep inside that Mya, their Sunrize, was tired.

"Sunrize, what do you want us to do?" she asked.

"Let's focus on the positive," Deranged replied.

"You guys, I've been out here alone—sometimes I'm participating alone, sometimes I'm riding alone—

and still I don't have the issues and altercations some of you have. You have got to learn to listen," Mya said with authority. Then she put her head down. "We have to make some changes. Who's participating? Who isn't? it's time to give your all! If you all agree, then let's get down to business! What's on the agenda?"

The meeting turned to regular business and the issues at hand were no longer an issue. The club began to engage on the other club issues.

"Annual dance, Sunrize," said Care Bear.

Grace nodded and said, "Let's focus on the important things, m'ija!" she added.

Everyone began to talk about the dance and to focus on the business at hand.

Back at home, Manny jumped right in on the club and how Bad Mamma-Jamma had misbehaved.

"I don't care what you say, that woman is too old to be cutting up like that! Y'all need to put her out the club!" he exclaimed. "I'm worried about your safety when you're with them!" he said firmly.

Mya listened and allowed him to go on and on while she prepared for bed. She always tried to hear his side of things, even though she could never truly understand his side because bike life was branded inside her and she wasn't about to let his opinions come between her and her biker family.

A few months went by and the day of the Ladies of Flavor Annual Dance had arrived. The ladies decided to do a luau theme since it was in the middle of July. Ladies of Flavor were known to throw some amazing events and each dance always had a twist. They could draw a decent crowd with P-Town's club always being the most in attendance. Clubs came from all around the city and Illinois. One of their favorite friends, G-Berry, came from North Carolina and showed much support. MC's, motorsports, social clubs, all were one big family at the annual dances. There were never any bad moments, and everyone was always organized, social, and ready to party.

Once the dance ended, as everyone was cleaning up, Manny pulled up on a new motorcycle he'd bought. It was the same kind as Mya's, a Hayabusa. She had taught him how to ride it only a few weeks prior to the dance.

"Y'all need any help?" he asked.

Mya smiled. "Sure," she said softly.

Some of her big brothers watched how she interacted with Manny and stood back in amazement.

G-Berry walked up to her and said, "Is this him, Sunrize? The one you're engaged to?" he asked again.

She nodded. "Yes, this is him."

Grace began to follow them and helped Manny as if she was keeping an eye on him. Grace was like that sometimes; she was very protective about her Sunrize. She stood back and also watched the couple.

The dance had gone well and the club had made a profit, which helped make sure the club stayed afloat to do more events.

Almost six months later, another mother-daughter duo had joined, and by this time, Desiree (PYT) was riding like a champ alongside her mother and was voted as the new road captain replacing Isis, whom they had not seen nor heard from in quite some time. Candy had fallen off dealing with some personal issues, and Mya was left with a lot of new people at one time.

Mya often thought about how fun it was when they were all together or when she, Isis, and Baby B rode until they were dead tired. They would get home sometimes and sleep like they were in a coma, but Mya was getting tired of the whole thing. She always compared herself to Otis from the Temptations. Everything for the club and nothing else.

*'Who else would sacrifice everything for the sake of the club as I have?'* she asked herself.

Mya had spent years keeping Ladies of Flavor alive, sacrificing time she could have shared with her children or family. The club was her baby. Yet, now Mya wanted to do some other things. She wanted to build her business, buy a home, take the kids on trips. She'd missed all that because there was always an event where she was needed to be, or one of the girls needed someone to ride with; sometimes they just needed someone to talk to. She always tried to be there for each and every one of them.

Manny got in trouble again with the law, causing Mya to measure the time she'd contributed to him to have more time to give out to the club. But he gave Mya an ultimatum: choose him or her bike life.

As she rode on her bike in thought, her choice was clear as she rode into the sunset...

*'He knew what I was when he met me, a biker chick!'*

www.ingramcontent.com/pod-product-compliance
Lightning Source LLC
Chambersburg PA
CBHW030151200626
46812CB00016B/1790